Welcome to Treeville
A Rugrats Christmas

by Jenny Migli...

illustrated by Sharon Ross

and Kevin Gallegly

SCHOLASTIC INC.

New York Toronto London Auckland Sydney
Mexico City New Delhi Hong Kong Buenos Aires

K L A S K Y
C S U P O INC.

Based on the TV series *Rugrats*® created by Arlene Klasky, Gabor Csupo, and
Paul Germain as seen on Nickelodeon®

ISBN 0-439-66681-3

12 11 10 9 8 7 6 5 4 3 2 1   4 5 6 7 8 9/0

Printed in the U.S.A.   23

First Scholastic printing, November 2004

It was the day before Christmas.

The babies and their families went
to buy a Christmas tree.
"Welcome to Treeville!" said a
worker dressed as an elf. He handed
each of the babies a bag of cookies.

"Let's find the bestest tree ever!"
Tommy said.
The others began to follow Tommy,
but a sign caught Angelica's eye.

"I have a better idea," Angelica said.
"Let's find Santa!"
The babies quickly agreed,
but Chuckie did not.

"That forest looks scary,"
Chuckie said. "What if we get lost?"
"We can leave a trail of cookies!"
Kimi said.

Lil held her cookies tightly.
"But we love Christmas cookies!"
she cried.
Phil picked up a cookie that he
had dropped.
"Even dirty ones," he said.

"We can drop my cookies,"
Chuckie said.
"Okay! To the workshop!"
Tommy said.
He took the lead.
The others followed.

The babies entered the forest.
Angelica ate all of her cookies.
She was still hungry.
"I bet Chuckie would not mind
if I ate one of his cookies,"
she said.

"Yum!" Angelica said. She ate another cookie and another. Soon, Chuckie's cookie trail was gone!

"I am hungry," Phil said. "Chuckie,
do you have any cookies left?"

12

"I just dropped my last one,"
Chuckie said.
He turned around and gasped.
"My cookies!" he cried.
"They are gone!"

Angelica was licking her fingers.
"Angelica!" Tommy shouted.
"You ate our cookie trail!"
Chuckie groaned. "We are lost!"

Angelica looked guilty.
Then she looked green.
"I do not feel so well," she moaned,
holding her stomach.
"I never want to see another
Christmas cookie again."

Then it started to snow.
It snowed and snowed.
"Brrr!" Lil shivered.
"I wish I had mittens."
"Me too," Phil said.

Kimi took a step and sunk
into the snow.
"I wish I had snow boots," she said.
"My feet are cold!"
"I wish I had a whistle,"
Tommy said. "Someone would
hear it and rescue us."

The sun began to set.
"It is getting dark,"
Chuckie said.
"I wish I had a flashlight."

19

"The only thing I wish for
is a cell phone," Angelica said.
"We would be saved in no time."
Just then the babies heard
a ringing sound.

"Listen!" Tommy cried.
"Angelica's wish came true!"
But it was not the sound
of a cell phone ringing.

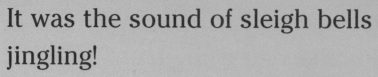

It was the sound of sleigh bells
jingling!
"Ho, ho, ho!" said a jolly man
with a white beard and a red suit.
"Santa!" the babies cried.

"You found my workshop,"
Santa said.
The babies looked puzzled.
Santa pointed to a house
above a snowy hill.

The house was Santa's
workshop!
There were toys everywhere.

"Toys!" Angelica cried. "Santa,
did you get my wish lists?"
"Yes, all nine of them," Santa said.
"Nine?" Angelica gasped. She
pulled a piece of paper from
her pocket.
"Oh, here is number ten."

Santa gave each of the babies
a candy cane.
"I must bring you back now,"
he said. "The elves and I have
a lot of work to do tonight."
The babies got on to Santa's sleigh.
They took off into the sky.

Soon the babies were
dropped off near their parents.
Quick as a wink, Santa was gone.
Stu and Chas were sawing the
trunk of a big tree.
Didi was planting a tree nearby.

"That is the best tree ever!"
Tommy cried.
Tommy's mom spun around.
"There you are!" she said.
"Were you playing hide and seek?"
The babies nodded.

"It's a shame Santa's Workshop is closed today," Kira said.
"The kids would have enjoyed it."
The babies looked at one another.
"Could it have all been a dream?" Tommy asked.

The next morning everyone met
for Christmas breakfast.
The babies opened their presents.
Phil and Lil got mittens.
Kimi got new snow boots.
Chuckie unwrapped his present.
"Wow! My own flashlight!"

Tommy pressed a shiny silver whistle between his lips. *"Toot, toot, toot!"* he squeaked happily.

"I bet I got a state-of-the-art cell . . ." Angelica stopped short. "COOKIES!" she shouted.

Just then the sound of sleigh bells could be heard.

"Ho, ho, ho!" Santa bellowed. "Merry Christmas!"